D0536950

CALGARY PUBLIC LIBRARY

NOV - 2011

Back to School Tortoise

Written by
Lucy M. George

Illustrated by
Merel Eyckerman

Albert Whitman & Company
Chicago, Illinois

Summer was almost over.

It was time to go
back to school.

Tortoise got up,

got dressed,

and had
breakfast.

Then he left
for school.

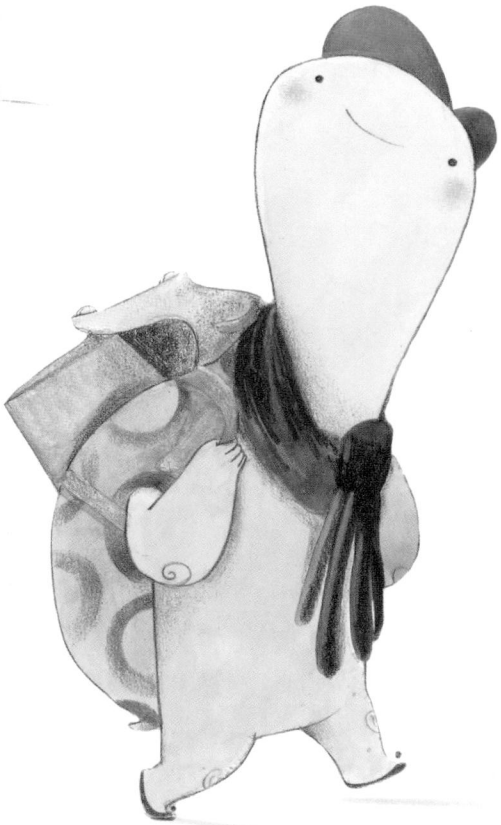

But he started
thinking,

what if...

...he tripped and fell?

Or he didn't like lunch?

Or the kids were mean to him?

What if he tripped
while getting lunch,

and all the kids
were mean to him?

"No," he decided.
"I can't go in."

He sat down
by the door.

But then he
started thinking,
what if...

...it was fun?

Or lunch was his favorite?

Or he made lots of new friends?

What if it was fun eating
his favorite lunch,

with all his new friends?

"I'll go to school!" he decided.

He took a
deep breath,

and opened
the door...

"Good morning, everyone!"

Tortoise said, as bravely as he could.

"Good morning,
Mr. Tortoise!"

they all shouted back.

For Mr. and Mrs. Andrews

L.M.G.

For everyone!

M.E.

The CIP record is available from the Library of Congress.

Text copyright © 2010 Lucy M. George.
Illustrations copyright © 2010 Merel Eyckerman.
First published in Great Britain by Meadowside Children's books.
Published in 2011 by Albert Whitman & Company.

ISBN 978-0-8075-0510-6

All rights reserved. No part of this book may be reproduced or transmitted in any form or by any means, electronic or mechanical, including photocopying, recording, or by any information storage and retrieval system, without permission in writing from the publisher. Printed in China.

10 9 8 7 6 5 4 3 2 SF 15 14 13 12 11 10

For more information about Albert Whitman & Company, visit our web site at www.albertwhitman.com.